TAKE ME OUT TO THE
BAT AND BALL
FACTORY

WRITTEN BY

Peggy Thomson

ILLUSTRATED BY

Gloria Kamen

Albert Whitman & Company

Morton Grove, Illinois

For swatters all—Mikey, Jamie of the "Rockies," Justine, Kyra, Maddie, and Concord High's Rookie of the Year, Angus. —P. T.

To all young baseball lovers, and especially to Alisa, Nathan, Ethan, and Daniel. —G. K.

It was to Worth, Inc., in Tullahoma, Tennessee, that we went in order to see wooden bats, aluminum bats, and balls, too, in the making—a triple treat, unique to this famous manufacturer of baseball equipment. Worth, Inc., has pioneered in many ways, including the manufacture of the RIF (reduced injury factor) baseball, used in youth leagues. Although most of its baseball stitching is now done overseas and although Worth, Inc.—since our visit—has quit making wood bats, its friendly guides were able to show us all the tools, machines, and processes that are used to produce the company's bats and balls. Our warm thanks to those guides and to the skilled workers, who take such pride and pleasure in their jobs.

Thanks, too, to Tom Bednark of the father-and-son Barnstable Bat Company on Cape Cod who gave us a special review course in the custom making of wood bats. Thanks to Washington, D.C.'s own baseball encyclopedia, writer Paul Dickson; to sports expert David Kelly at the Library of Congress; and to baseball fans/players/coaches Tom Fredenburg, David Thomson, McSlugger Ann McEwen, John Heidemann, and Matt and Stanley Namovicz.

Library of Congress Cataloging-in-Publication Data
Thomson, Peggy
Take me out to the bat and ball factory / by Peggy Thomson; illustrated by Gloria Kamen.
p. cm.
Summary: Describes how baseballs and bats are made, marked, and used.
ISBN 0-8075-7737-5
1. Baseball—United States—Equipment and supplies—Juvenile literature.
[1. Baseball—Equipment and supplies.] I. Kamen, Gloria, ill. II. Title.
GV879.7.T48 1998 688.7'6357'0973—dc21 97-27877
CIP   AC

Bats and balls! Bats that you swing, and *crack!* it's a hit! Balls that you hit, and it's over the fence!

Hank's factory makes them by the millions. They'll be used by boys, girls, and grown-ups, for playing catch, baseball, T-ball, and softball, in the ballparks, in yards and alleys, on playgrounds.

"Welcome!" says Hank. "We've got skills to show, and lots of stuff—wood, aluminum, leather, chemicals—tools, too, and big machines. It's a noisy place to work, full of sparks and sawdust—lots of sawdust—and many smells. We love it.

"Let's start with the wood bats."

Bats were once made from hickory wood so people called them "hickory sticks" or "old hickories." Now most wooden bats are made of Northern white ash. Ash is hard, lightweight, and has a good spring to it.

Wood Bats

"Here," says Hank, "in this warm, dry shed called a *kiln*, the bats aren't bats yet. They're still *billets*—big rounds of wood in rough baseball-bat sizes.

"We keep them drying for a few months. Then these great stacks of billets are ready to be whittled down into bats."

"Even before the billets are cut, some ballplayers come right here to our kiln room to get first choice. They know the color and grain of wood they want.

"Players want a bat to be big and light—big so it hits every ball, light so they can swing it fast. We say, 'You can't have it both ways,' but then we try, anyhow."

The light grain in a bat is the strong, dense wood—from the tree's spring growth. The dark grain—from summer growth—is porous. It has little holes in it. When a bat breaks, it breaks in the dark grain.

Little pin knots are okay in a bat—Babe Ruth really liked them—but big ones will weaken it.

"Now the bat rides to the sanding machines. The operator runs the sander with a foot pedal. The bat spins one way, sandpaper the other. Then it's into the cut-off saw to remove the handles. And a real bat rolls down the ramp."

Sander

cut

cut

MODERN BATS ARE LIGHTER THAN OLD-TIME BATS— THINNER THROUGH THE HANDLE AND BARREL.

I'M GLAD MY BAT'S LIGHT.

A rule was made in 1895 that bats have to be completely round—no flat surfaces are allowed on them. For the major leagues, all bats must be made of wood and cannot be longer than 42 inches, or wider than 2 and 3/4 inches.

I BURNED A FEW BATS, LEARNING.

"We put some bats through a hoop of flames to darken the dark grain of the wood. That's for players who want their bats to look dramatic.

"Some big league players keep a pattern bat here on a special rack. Some of them use a new bat for every game. Others use a lucky bat over and over. And every new bat has to be just like the pattern bat or it throws off their swing. Half an ounce too heavy—even less—and they won't use it."

Some players send back a bat for another spin at the lathe. They say: make it a shade thinner, a whisker lighter. The lathe operator has to figure it out.

At Hank's factory, great numbers of hanging bats travel around the huge finishing room, riding high, then dipping into tanks for baths in colors or in clear varnish.

One stop along the ride is for bright lettering and a trademark to be stenciled onto the barrel of the bat. Another stop is for a number to be stamped on the end of the handle, showing how many inches long the bat is—32, say, or 34.

"Now these wood bats are dry and ready to go," says Hank. "And we did it—900 beautiful bats before lunch!"

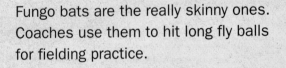

Fungo bats are the really skinny ones. Coaches use them to hit long fly balls for fielding practice.

Aluminum Bats

"Making aluminum bats is different," Hank says. "The bats start out hollow—they're tubes that go through *swagers* (SWAY-jers) and get pressed into shape.

"Inside the swagers, *dies* do the job. They're heavy metal blocks with carved-out bat shapes. The tube and the dies spin around. And hammers put on huge pressure—500,000 pounds of it, like the weight of 25 dump trucks.

"After a trip through two swagers, the tube comes out with a barrel end and a long, thin handle. The aluminum has been stretched to less than 1/12 of an inch thick."

THE BIG SQUEEZE— IM*PRESS*IVE!

"The aluminum is still strong, but now it has a bit of bend to it. Picture a pitch, the ball connects, *sproing!*— it bounces off on a fast ride. The bat is a trampoline.

"Our bat makes one trip now through the saw. Metal cuts metal to get the right length for each bat. Then it goes to the spinner where the wide end of the bat is spun partway closed."

SHRIEK!

"Perfect," says Hank. "Here we pack the bats onto our big batcatcher rolling carts. And we send the bats away to be *anodized*. When they come back to us, the aluminum has been changed. Our bats are dazzling. They've taken on colors and a shine, like soda cans, with catchy names and bright designs."

WRITE IT BIG AND CLEAR— HANK'S BATS!

RED ON SILVER...

...ON SHINY BLACK!

"Our fancy bat is still hollow. So we fit a boot over the big end to stop any leaks, and then fill the bat with a thick gooey plastic called *polyurethane* that foams and gels and turns hard. The worker controls the flow with her foot pedal. Look out! Not too full!"

POINK

"That filler is for weight," Hank says. "And it tunes the bat, too. When a ball is hit, there needs to be a great ringing *poink!* like the *crack!* from a wood bat. *Crack!* and *poink!* are the power sounds of baseball."

GRINDING

ZZZZ

WELDING

BUFFING

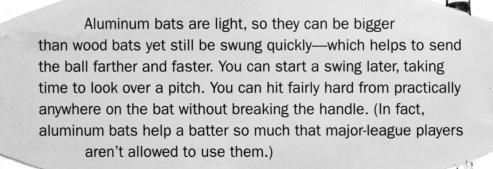

Aluminum bats are light, so they can be bigger than wood bats yet still be swung quickly—which helps to send the ball farther and faster. You can start a swing later, taking time to look over a pitch. You can hit fairly hard from practically anywhere on the bat without breaking the handle. (In fact, aluminum bats help a batter so much that major-league players aren't allowed to use them.)

WRAPPING GRIPS AND LABELLING

"From here things move fast. A grinder grinds the bat's handle smooth. A welder welds on the knob, with sparks flying. A buffer buffs it on a wheel.

"Wrappers wrap grips onto the handle and drop each finished bat into a cart. Then we label and pack and ship the bats all over the country—to games and good times," says Hank.

TAGGING AND PACKAGING

Players do love their bats! When Babe Ruth traveled, he let other people carry his baggage, but never his bag of bats. He carried that.

When Ted Williams finished the 1941 season with his amazing .406 batting average, he gave his bat a big kiss!

Bats & Batting

Joe DiMaggio

As a kid playing on a sandlot, **Joe DiMaggio** batted with his fisherman father's broken oar. He was six when he started playing.

Stan Musial

Stan Musial got laughs for holding his bat like a flyswatter.

Kirby Puckett, when he was in a batting slump, practiced his swings to music in his living room.

The Padres' all-star hitter **Tony Gwynn** gets his hits from his extra-small bat—just 29 inches long.

Henry (Hank) Aaron

Hank Aaron, as a kid, batted bottlecaps with a broomstick. He later said this was good practice because bottlecaps dip and float like curveballs. For years he batted cross-handed. No one corrected him until he was a pro.

Left-handed batter **Babe Ruth** held his bat at the very end, with the knob of the bat in his right hand. His batting system: "I pick a good one and sock it."

Mickey Mantle

Ty Cobb's lifetime batting average was the highest ever—.367.

Babe Ruth

Mickey Mantle's father pitched to him left-handed—so Mantle batted right-handed. His grandfather pitched to him right-handed—so Mantle batted left-handed. Mantle grew up to be the best switch-hitter of his day.

Roberto Clemente

Ken Griffey Jr.

Roberto Clemente got his first bat from a guava-tree branch.

In their first at-bats, as teammates for the Seattle Mariners, Ken Griffey and his son **Ken Griffey, Junior,** each hit the second pitch for a single. Just weeks later, they hit back-to-back home runs.

Balls

"Onward!" says Hank, "to where we make the balls. To make balls, you need cores and covers. And you need good stitching to hold everything together.

"Start with the cores—the bouncy innards of the balls. The cores we produce here are made of the same polyurethane that's inside the aluminum bats. The cores get their shape from molds.

"Here at our big carousels, metal molds make slow trips, going around and around."

1 PREPARING THE MIX

2 FILLING THE MOLD

3 POPPING OPEN THE MOL REM THE C

If the chemistry is wrong, then the bounce is off, and the ball won't be as lively as it ought to be. To make two cores, it takes 1/2 cup of resin and 1/4 cup of hardener.

"Workers on the job spray the molds with wax to keep them slick. They fill each mold with the liquid and clamp it into the carousel for its ride. Inside the molds, the runny mixture expands and gives off heat. It turns custardy, gooey, stringy. It gels and goes hard. Then one worker called a *puller* sprays air into each mold to open the lid and pop out the core. Now the core is a ball shape. It better be! She stamps a date on it and drops it onto a rack. All the just-right cores are tossed into buggies, to be hauled away."

NOW FOR THE STITCHING...

CORES COME IN DIFFERENT COLORS, TO TELL DIFFERENT BATCHES APART.

"Covers for the balls are made of leather—either natural or fake. Almost all of it is white, but some is grayish," says Hank. "And some is even bright blue, red, orange—for balls you can see when you're playing in snow.

"We lay out a long sheet of vinyl—fake leather—on a table, and put our clicker on top of it. That's our cutting machine with a sharp steel die for stamping out a batch of ball covers. Cookie-cutter work is what it is.

"It takes two pieces to cover a ball. Together, the pieces wrap around the core. No overlapping! No gaps either!"

LACY LEFTOVERS!

THAT MEANS THERE'S NOT MUCH WASTE.

TINY HOLES AROUND THE EDGES SHOW WHERE TO STITCH. AND EXTRA-TINY HOLES SHOW WHERE TO START.

TWO LENGTHS OF RED THREAD

MACHINES NEVER STITCH A BALL RIGHT. THEY MAKE A MESS OF IT.

"The cores are just slightly sticky," says Hank, "because we've dipped them in a special glue.

"That helps the stitcher. Meet Jean. She cups the two cover pieces around a core. She matches up the tiny holes and staples the covers to the core just to keep the covers from slipping while she works.

"Jean measures the thread— about twice her outstretched arms— and cuts it. It's red cotton thread— waxy to help it slide. She threads a needle onto each end, and starts stitching. Left needle, right needle— like lacing a shoe."

"My stepmother stitched balls on our front porch," Jean remembers. "She taught me when I was twelve. When you're a beginner, it takes 45 minutes a ball. Then you get it down to 10 or 8 minutes. A baseball has 108 stitches. A softball is bigger but has only 88. All the stitching is one long, snaky seam."

STAPLING

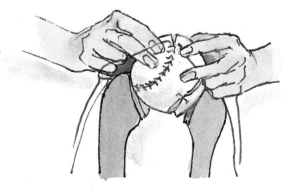

STITCHING

Hank's balls are used just about anywhere, except in the major leagues. Major league baseballs have to be 9 to 9 1/4 inches around and weigh 5 to 5 1/4 ounces. The cores are rubber-coated cork, wound around with yarns. Since 1974, the covers have been cowhide. Before that, they were horsehide, and people called balls "old horsehides." Since 1934, the stitching has had to be red.

REALLY EARLY BALLS HAD SHEEPSKIN COVERS AND—OUCH!—SOME BALLS HAD LEAD IN THE CENTER.

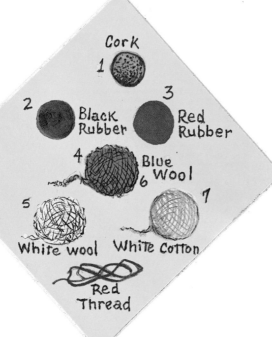

Cork
1
2 Black Rubber
3 Red Rubber
4
Blue Wool
6
5
7
White wool   White Cotton
Red Thread

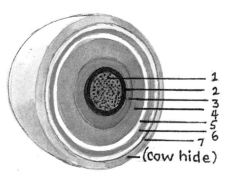

1
2
3
4
5
6
7
(cow hide)

Softballs are 12 inches around. They weigh 12 ounces, and they aren't soft. They're just about as hard as baseballs.

Sometimes you want a ball that won't fly far. That's why Hank makes some balls as big around as grapefruits.

A new type of baseball has a safety feature. If a fastball hits a player, the core flattens out enough to soften the blow.

“We’re on the move now,” says Hank, “to where our winches lift the buggies full of balls and dump out the loads. Washers wash and buff. Stampers feed one ball at a time into the stamping machine for a logo—names, numbers, designs.”

“Packers stack the balls in rows of pyramids to dry. And boxers drop the balls into cartons for shipping. We all think we’re speedy,” says Hank, “but the boxers have the fastest hands in the factory.”

Balls and Pitching

Walter
Johnson

Walter Johnson's fastball blew by so fast it was called a pneumonia ball for its icy wind. It was so fast that batters sometimes closed their eyes.

Satchel Paige's fastball was his trouble ball, his shadowball, or his "bee" ball, "because it would always be where I wanted it to be."

Satchel
Paige

Lopsiders: In early baseball, one ball was expected to last through a game; somewhat later, two. In the course of play, balls got mushy, sometimes ripped and lopsided, and the "mush balls" no longer traveled as far. At least one one-ball ball game was still played in 1908.

Nolan Ryan's fastball, the Ryan Express, was sometimes clocked at more than 100 miles an hour. Ryan as a Texas kid developed fast hands— rolling, tying, stacking newspapers. He liked to throw—sometimes rocks at poisonous snakes.

Nolan
Ryan

The Cardinals' **Dizzy Dean** said about his pitching: "I just rear back and fog 'em through."

One pitcher said pitching a fastball to record-breaking batter **Hank Aaron** was like trying to sneak the sun past a rooster.

Right-hander **Roger Clemens**, "Rocket Man," holds the major league record because he has twice struck out 20 players in a nine-inning game. Mariners' **Randy Johnson**, called "the Big Unit" for his six-foot ten-inch frame, has twice struck out 19 players—the record for a left hander.

It's a help to pitchers to have big hands. Dodgers pitcher **Sandy Koufax** could hold 5 baseballs in his hand at one time.

Mudballs: Before major league games, umpires rub up six dozen baseballs with a special rubbing mud. That's so the balls won't be too slick or glary-white. And any time the ball hits the ground, the umpire examines it for scuffs or nicks. The pitcher checks, too. If the ball doesn't feel right, he asks for another. The average life for a ball: six pitches.

Cy Young, who played from 1890-1911, won the most games of any major league pitcher—511. The annual award for the best pitcher in each league is named for him. And **Greg Maddux** of the Atlanta Braves, known for his control and savvy, has won the Cy Young Award four times in a row.

Hank's History of Baseball

1816

NEW YORK KNICKERBOCKERS

1863

1869

CINCINNATI RED STOCKINGS

Rounders came first—an English bat-and-ball game. It came to the New World with settlers and adventurers, and sometimes it was even called *base ball*. We know because "B is for Base-Ball" is the first line of a poem in a book from 1744.

In the 1700s and early 1800s, base ball was popular in New England. It had other names, too—goal ball, Indian ball, and one old cat. You had one base, and—to put a runner out—you hit him with a thrown ball.

Then there was town ball, a game that's still played at the Baseball Museum in Cooperstown, New York, right by the Baseball Hall of Fame. The ball is black, made of one piece of leather. You run the bases—four of them—in any order, dodging the thrown ball, while fans yell:

"Soak 'im! Plug 'im!"

In New York City, a man named Alexander Cartwright and his friends played a new way. Nine players on a team. Three tries for a hit. No more throwing at a runner. And one day Cartwright plotted out a diamond the way it is today. He paced off 42 paces—90 feet—between the bases.

Cartwright started the Knickerbocker Base Ball Club of New York. The first game was in 1846. The Knickerbockers lost, 23 to 1, and one player was fined six cents—for swearing.

Later, Cartwright headed west, spreading news of baseball. During the Civil War, soldiers on both sides—North and South—played the game in their free time.

All this came before the major leagues and the World Series.

Before Little League and softball, before baseball cards and uniforms with numbers and batting helmets (in other words, before baseball as we know it).

In 1869, the Cincinnati Red Stockings were the first team to pay their players. The National League was formed in 1876; the American League in 1900. And over the years, baseball just went big and bigger—with more teams and players, with crowds of fans. It came to be called "the national pastime."

Once, in 1910, while President Taft was attending a game, he happened to stand up between halves of the seventh inning. He was just restless. And then other fans in the stands stood up, too, to be respectful to the president. And that was the start of a tradition—the seventh-inning stretch.

That was before the 1920s, the era of the new lively ball (it had tighter winding and traveled farther), the years that belonged to left-handed slugger Babe Ruth,

The Bambino   The Sultan of Swat

with his famous 714—count 'em—home runs and his skinny-legged trot around the bases, waving his cap to the crowds as he rounded third.

That was before the magic numbers 56 and 406, in 1941.

**When Joe DiMaggio hit safely in 56 games in a row.
And Ted Williams had his .406 batting average.**

During World War II, women played professional baseball on teams named the Belles, Peaches, Blue Sox, Daisies, Redwings, and Chicks. And they played a tough, fast game.

From 1920 the Negro leagues had flourished, playing to big crowds, but it was not until April 15, 1947, that major league ball finally opened up to black players as well as white. On that great day, Jackie Robinson walked out on the field to play second base for the Dodgers. He was a terrific player who loved the game, and he had the guts not to fight back when he was hit with boos, ugly talk, and threats. That year he won the first Rookie of the Year Award. He'd already won the hearts of fans and the confidence of other players.

1876

NATIONAL LEAGUE FORMED

1910

WILLIAM HOWARD TAFT

1943

PEACHES, BLUE SOX

April 8, 1974 was another big day.

That was when Hank Aaron hit his 715th home run and beat Babe Ruth's all-time record.

In all, Hammerin' Hank hit 755 home runs. (And don't forget his 714th was the first cowhide home run.)

In that same year, Little League, which had been only for boys since it began in 1939, opened up to welcome girl players, too. Carl Yastrzemski of the Red Sox was the first former Little Leaguer to be elected to baseball's Hall of Fame. And especially don't forget 2030 and 2031, in 1996...

When the Orioles' Cal Ripken broke Lou Gehrig's record of playing in 2030 consecutive games.

The celebrated Ripken hadn't missed a game in 13 years.

In 1997: 50 years since Jackie Robinson's first game! All honor to famous jersey number 42! In 1997: suspense, too. Mark McGwire with 58 homers, and Ken Griffey, Jr., with 56 chased Roger Maris's record of 61 in '61 and Babe Ruth's 60 in '27, 59 in '21. They came close.

Who knows what records and numbers will amaze us next? Time will tell.

LITTLE LEAGUE OPENS TO GIRLS 1974

JACKIE ROBINSON

SO, HANK, ISN'T IT TIME...

...TO PLAY BALL?

I'LL PITCH!

I'LL SHAG!

SHAG MEANS T FETCH—CH AND CATC FLY BALLS PART OF BATTING PRACTIC